Disney · PIXAR

TOY STORY

Advance
PUBLISHERS

Andy and Sheriff Woody were the best of friends. It didn't matter that Andy was a boy and Woody was a toy. When you had been through the kinds of adventures these two had shared—fighting bad guys, saving the day, and riding off into the sunset together too many times to count—well, you developed an unbreakable, unshakeable bond.

Andy had other toys he liked to play with too. But Woody was number one, the big cheese, the top dog. And because of that, Woody had a place of honor on Andy's bed.

On this particular day, Andy dropped Woody off in his usual spot. "It's party time!" Andy shouted happily, scooping up his little sister Molly, "See you later, Woody!"

The room was very quiet for a few seconds—and then Woody sat up! "Okay everybody, coast is clear!" he shouted.

Toys peeked out from the closet, climbed out of the toy chest, and scrambled out from under the bed. Mr. Potato Head, Hamm, Slinky Dog, R.C., Rex, and Bo Peep continued a conversation they'd been having the last time there were no people around to hear them.

But Woody didn't have time to chat. He had important news. Andy's family (and all of his toys) would be moving to a new house the following week, so Andy's birthday party had been rescheduled—for today!

Every kid needs a place to dream. It doesn't matter how big or small the place is. Although Andy shares a room with his sister, Molly, the tiny tot can't walk yet. That means Andy has the floor space to himself and can happily spend hours playing games with his toys.

This wasn't happy news. The toys all dreaded Andy's birthdays. They were afraid that some cool new present would arrive to take their place. And this year—on this particular birthday—their worst fears were realized. Andy got the coolest toy ever!

His name was Buzz Lightyear, and he told the other toys he was a space ranger who had just landed on Earth. He also told them he could fly. "To infinity and beyond!" Buzz shouted, launching himself from the bed and bouncing off a ball high into the air.

The other toys ooohed and aaahed, but Woody wasn't impressed.

"That's not flying," he insisted. "That's just falling with style."

Woody is not happy when Buzz arrives. First, Andy knocks Woody under the bed and gives Buzz his spot on top. Then, to make matters worse, the other toys are blown away by the space ranger's gadgetry. Woody is worried about losing Andy, and he's definitely feeling some toy rivalry.

After Buzz arrived, things just weren't the same. Andy was still fighting bad guys and saving the day—but now he was doing it with Buzz instead of Woody. The other toys all wanted to spend their time with Buzz too. Worst of all, Buzz now had the position of honor on Andy's bed—and Woody felt forlorn and forgotten.

So when Woody heard that Andy could choose only one toy to take to Pizza Planet one night, he decided to make sure Andy chose him. Woody tried to push Buzz behind the desk where Andy wouldn't find him—but Buzz fell out the window instead!

The other toys thought Woody had pushed Buzz out the window on purpose. "Didn't want to face the fact that Buzz just might be Andy's new favorite toy, so you got rid of him!" Mr. Potato Head accused Woody.

Just then, Andy dashed into the room. He looked everywhere for Buzz, but when he couldn't find him, he grabbed Woody instead and ran outside. As Andy hopped into the car, a small figure grabbed onto the car's bumper and held on for all it was worth.

When Andy and his mom got out of the car at a gas station on the way to Pizza Planet, Buzz leaped into the back seat with Woody. Even though Woody denied it, Buzz didn't believe that his fall had been an accident.

"You tried to terminate me, but revenge is not an idea we promote on my planet," Buzz said, narrowing his eyes menacingly, "We're not on my planet though, are we?" With that, Buzz tackled Woody. As the toys wrestled and wrangled, they fell out of the car—and Andy's mom drove away without them!

They were stranded. Buzz insisted that he was going to find a way back to his home planet. Woody argued that Buzz was a toy, not a space ranger, and his place was with Andy. When a Pizza Planet delivery truck pulled into the gas station, Woody had an idea.

Hamm and his pal Mr. Potato Head enjoy beating each other in friendly games of poker. They are playing cards when Buzz falls out the window, and for once Hamm doesn't care if he holds the winning hand.

Woody knew he couldn't go home and face the other toys without Buzz. He told Buzz that the Pizza Planet truck would take them to a spaceport, where Buzz could get a ride back to his planet. Woody figured if they could just catch up with Andy, all would be well.

When they got to Pizza Planet, Woody spotted Andy and his family. Woody signaled Buzz to jump into Molly's stroller, but when he turned around, Buzz wasn't there! Buzz had spotted a rocket ship that looked like it could take him home.

The three-eyed Aliens in the crane game at Pizza Planet believe "The Claw" is their master. "It chooses who will go and who will stay," they chant. As Woody tries to pull Buzz to safety, the Aliens gang up on him.

Before Woody could stop him, Buzz had climbed into the Rocket Ship Crane Game. Woody scrambled in after him. He had to find a way to convince Buzz to come home. Before either of them realized what was happening, the machine started whirring and a big silver claw dropped onto Buzz.

As the crane tugged at Buzz, Woody grabbed onto Buzz's feet and tried to free him. But both toys were lifted up and dropped into the prize slot.

"All right! Double prizes!" gloated the boy who was operating the claw. Woody realized with horror that the boy was Andy's nasty toy-torturing neighbor, Sid.

Sid took Buzz and Woody home to his dark, creepy room filled with scary tools for his infamous toy "operations." Left alone in the gloom, Buzz and Woody heard strange rustling and shifting sounds. As they watched in terror, the toy mutants Sid had created from his once-normal toys crept out from the shadows.

Seeing a chance to escape the horrors of that room, Buzz and Woody raced out into the hall—right into Sid's vicious dog, Scud.

Fleeing the dog, Woody and Buzz ran in different directions. Buzz heard a voice shouting, "Calling Buzz Lightyear! This is Star Command!"

Buzz was about to respond when the voice continued, "The world's greatest superhero, now the world's greatest toy!" Buzz listened in shock as the voice on the TV added, "Not a flying toy."

Suddenly Buzz questioned everything he had believed about himself—that he was a space ranger, that he could fly. Not willing to accept what he had just heard, Buzz went out into the hallway, climbed to the top of the stair railing, spread his wings—and leaped! "To infinity and beyond!" Buzz shouted. And then he dropped to the ground.

The leader of the mutant toys, Babyface is a doll head on top of a spider like body made from construction set pieces. She lives in the shadows under Sid's bed and creeps across the floor like a spider. She uses her crab like pinchers to bang out Morse code on Sid's bed to call the other toys from their hiding places.

Buzz's left arm was broken off in the fall—but even more serious than that, Buzz's spirit was broken too. He wasn't a superhero, he wasn't a space ranger—he was nothing more than a toy. A toy!

Buzz lost his will to fight. He just didn't care anymore—he refused to do anything to save himself. Desperate to save them both, Woody tried to get help from Andy's toys next door. But Buzz wouldn't even come to the window, and when Andy's toys spied Buzz's loose arm, they assumed that Woody had hurt Buzz. Woody was on his own.

Woody didn't think things could get much worse—but then he realized that the mutant toys in Sid's room had surrounded Buzz! Woody tried to fight them off, but they took Buzz's broken arm and firmly pushed Woody away.

Moments later, the toys stepped away from Buzz. Buzz didn't look hurt, in fact Buzz looked as good as new. The mutant toys had reattached Buzz's arm! They weren't the bad guys after all—they were on Woody's side!

When he's not exploding toys, Sid enjoys tearing them apart and recombining them in strange and frightening ways. When Sid captures Buzz and Woody with the Claw at Pizza Planet, Woody is sure they are doomed. No toy ever escapes from Sid's house.

The toys scattered suddenly when they heard Sid stomping up the stairs. Only Buzz stayed where he was—he still didn't care what happened to him.

Sid strapped a rocket to Buzz's back for blast off the next morning. All night long, Woody tried to talk Buzz into escaping. "Over in that house is a kid who thinks you are the greatest. And it's not because you're a space ranger. It's because you're his toy," Woody said. "You are a cool toy!"

By the time Buzz finally realized that Woody was right—that being Andy's toy really was important—it was too late. It was almost time for blast off!

But Woody had a plan. He and all of Sid's toys would have to break some rules. If it worked though, it would be a victory for toys everywhere.

Before Sid could light the rocket on Buzz's back, Woody and the other toys surrounded him. "From now on, you must take good care of your toys," Woody warned the stunned and terrified boy. "Because if you don't, we'll find out, Sid."

The toys were alive! And threatening him! Sid ran screaming in terror into the house. The toys cheered. Not only had they saved Buzz, but they knew that Sid would never dare to harm another toy.

Woody and Buzz didn't have time to celebrate. It was moving day, and if they didn't hurry, Andy's family would leave without them.

With the rocket still on his back, Buzz couldn't fit through the fence. He told Woody to leave him, but Woody refused to abandon his friend. Working together, Woody and Buzz finally escaped—just in time to see the moving van drive away!

Racing after the van, Buzz caught hold of a strap and pulled himself up onto the rear of the truck. He was trying to pull Woody up after him when Scud grabbed Woody from behind.

"Noooooo!" Buzz yelled, jumping off the van onto Scud's head.

Now Woody was on the van, and Buzz was in danger. Thinking quickly, Woody opened the back of the moving van and pulled R.C. out of one of the boxes. Using the remote control, Woody sent R.C. out to get Buzz.

The rest of Andy's toys still didn't trust Woody, so they pushed him off the van. But Buzz and R.C. picked up Woody as they sped past him, and the toys on the van finally understood that Woody and Buzz were working together.

All would have been well, but just then R.C.'s batteries ran out! R.C. slowed to a halt, and the three toys watched in distress as the moving van pulled further and further away.

Things looked hopeless until the toys realized that the rocket on Buzz's back could help. Once it was lit, the toys held onto each other, and the rocket catapulted them into the air. Buzz and Woody dropped R.C. into the open van with the other toys and then zoomed ahead to catch up with Andy in the family car.

Just as the rocket was about to explode, Buzz snapped open his wings and they broke free. "Buzz, you're flying!" Woody shouted excitedly.

"This isn't flying," Buzz shouted back as they soared through the sky, "This is falling with style!"

Every toy should have a kid like Andy to play with. He has energy and imagination to spare. He was sad when Woody and Buzz disappeared. When the missing toys show up in the car, Andy is very happy. He has no idea what the two toys had gone through to get home to him.

Buzz maneuvered skillfully until he and Woody were gliding right over the family's car. Then, while Andy was looking out the window, the toys dropped unnoticed through the open sun roof into a box on the back seat.

Hearing a thump, Andy looked into the box. "Woody! Buzz!" he exclaimed joyously when he saw his two favorite toys. Andy hugged them both hard—he had been so afraid that his good friends were lost forever. Now everything was right with the world, and the friends could all move into their new house—together.

Overcoming his jealousy, Woody convinces Buzz that being a child's favorite toy is a wonderful thing. As Buzz and Woody work together to escape from Sid and get back to Andy, they both learn that loyalty and friendship are more than just child's play.

After their adventures together, Buzz and Woody knew they could count on each other through thick and thin—which is why they were huddled together as Andy opened his presents that Christmas.

"You aren't worried, are you?" Woody asked Buzz.

"No, no," Buzz fibbed. "Are you?"

"Now Buzz," Woody said, teasing his good friend, "What could Andy possibly get that is worse than you?"

Just then, the toys heard a strange sound coming from the living room downstairs.

"Woof woof!"

"Wow! A puppy!" they heard Andy exclaim.

Buzz and Woody exchanged nervous grins. Uh-oh.

JOKES, RIDDLES, AND SILLY STUFF!

Here are some of my favorites

Knock. Knock.
Who's there?
Lasso.
Lasso who?
Lasso nice hat you got, cowgirl!

What do you call Rex when he wears cowboy boots?
Tyrannosaurus Tex.

What do you have to know to teach new tricks to an old horse?
More than the horse!

What did the cowboy say to the crayon?
Draw, pardner!

Where does a horse go shopping?
On Mane Street.

What do you get when you mix a telephone and a cowboy?
The phone ranger.

BO PEEP GIGGLES

Where does Bo Peep take her sheep for a haircut?
To the baa-baa shop.

Why do sheep never forget?
Because no one ever tells them anything.

Why can sheep always keep secrets?
You never get a peep out of them.

What's Hamm's favorite ballet?
Swine Lake.

What do you get if you cross bacon with a spaceship?
An unidentified frying object.

What do you say to a good-looking piggy bank?
Hi, Ham-some!

Where did Hamm go on Sunday?
To a pignic.

REX'S FAVORITE FUNNIES

What do you call Rex when he plays rodeo?
A bronco-saurus.

What do you get when you cross a dinosaur with a witch?
A tyrannosaurus hex.

How does Rex go to a Halloween party?
Dressed as a Terror-dactyl!

How do dinosaurs pay for things?
With Tyrannosaurus checks!

What did the doctor say to the invisible dinosaur?
I can't see you now.

What do you hear when Rex is sleeping?
A dino-snore!

How do you know if there's a dinosaur in the refrigerator?
Footprints in the pizza.